Barbie™
THE BIG SPLASH

By Barbara Slate
Illustrated by Tom Tierney

A GOLDEN BOOK • NEW YORK
Western Publishing Company, Inc., Racine, Wisconsin 53404

Barbie was enjoying a quiet afternoon in her apartment when the telephone rang. "Hello," said Barbie.

"Congratulations!" said the voice on the other end. "This is Karen Johns, editor of *What's In* magazine. You've been chosen to pose for the famous *What's In* swimsuit issue."

"That's great!" Barbie exclaimed. "It's an honor to be chosen."

Karen went on to explain that three models, including Barbie, would be flown to the luxurious island of Wanaumana for the shoot.

A week later, as she boarded the plane for
Wanaumana, Barbie recognized one of the other
models and introduced herself.

"Hi, I'm Barbie," she said. "I really enjoy your
commercials for Hidden Secret perfume."

"Thank you, Barbie," said the model. "I'm Estella,
and I really like your Jump Jeans commercials."

Barbie and Estella quickly became friends.

Barbie and Estella found Karen, the magazine
editor, on board the plane. Karen introduced them to
Skovoola, the world-famous photographer. Skovoola
was going to be photographing them for the
swimsuit issue.

Then Karen checked her list and noticed that
Laureen, the third model, hadn't boarded the
plane yet.

Just then, Laureen made a grand entrance.

"Dahlings, dahlings, I hope I'm not too late," she gushed.

Laureen walked right past Barbie and stopped in front of Skovoola.

"Oh, Skovoola," she chattered, "it's soooo wonderful to see you!"

"Good to see you, too, Laureen," the photographer responded.

Laureen sat down and opened her bag. She took out her compact and looked at herself in the mirror.

"It's nice to be in the swimsuit issue," Laureen thought. "But who's going to be on the cover? Estella got the cover the past two years. Karen will probably want a new look, so Barbie is my only real competition."

After the plane landed on Wanaumana, Barbie
and the others headed for the hotel.

The crew planned to spend the morning setting
up for the shoot. Karen gave the models their
schedules.

"Skovoola will be photographing Laureen this
afternoon," she said. "Barbie is tomorrow morning,
and Estella tomorrow afternoon."

Barbie was happy to have the day off. "I heard about a place on the other side of the island where you can swim with dolphins," she told Estella. "Would you like to go with me?"

Estella said she'd rather relax by the hotel pool and soak up some sun.

"Well, enjoy your day," said Barbie as she headed off.

Barbie found her way to Dolphin Cove on the other side of the island. Paul, a dolphin trainer, showed Barbie how to make friends with the animals.

"Put out your hand, Barbie," he said.

Barbie followed Paul's instructions, and the dolphins began to swim up to her. One dolphin put his head close to Barbie's face.

"That's Herman," said Paul. "He wants you to pat him."

Barbie gently patted the top of Herman's head.

"Now lift your hand and wave to Herman," Paul instructed.

When Barbie waved, Herman waved back with his flippers. Barbie laughed happily as Herman splashed water all around her. She spent the rest of the afternoon swimming with Herman. When she left, Barbie really felt as though she had made a new friend.

The next morning Barbie was up at dawn to prepare for her photo shoot.

The hairdresser washed and set Barbie's hair. Then she brushed it out for a natural look. After that, the makeup artist went to work. The stylist brought out the bathing suit Barbie would be modeling.

Soon Skovoola was photographing Barbie
running on the beach,

listening to a seashell,

and playing in the ocean.

Laureen, the jealous model who wanted to be chosen for the cover of *What's In,* was watching from behind some bushes. "Barbie is a great model," she thought. "Too great. If I don't act fast, she will get the cover for sure!"

When Barbie's shoot was over, Skovoola took the roll of film out of his camera and put it into his photo bag. Then he went over to talk to Estella about the next shoot.

"Now's my chance," thought Laureen as Skovoola turned away. With no one looking, Laureen edged her way toward Skovoola's photo bag and took the film. Then she dropped it into her beach bag and disappeared again behind the bushes.

Laureen smiled to herself. With Barbie out of the way, she was a shoo-in for the cover.

After the photo shoot with Estella, Skovoola
looked into his bag and saw that the film of Barbie
was missing. Skovoola was frantic.

"This is our last day on the island," said Karen.
"If we don't photograph Barbie again this afternoon,
we won't have any pictures of her!"

"But where is she?" asked Skovoola.

"I think I know," said Estella. "Let's go get her."

Estella led everyone to Dolphin Cove. There was Barbie, busy playing with Herman. She didn't notice her friends calling to her from the shore.

"Wow!" cried Skovoola. "I've never photographed a dolphin before."

Soon Skovoola was snapping pictures of Herman.
"Oh, dear," Karen fretted. "The sunlight is fading.
Without it, we'll never be able to get any more
pictures of Barbie!"

Herman swam underneath Barbie and playfully
lifted her out of the water. Barbie looked beautiful
as she rose out of the bright blue ocean.

When she noticed that it was getting late, Barbie swam to shore. She was surprised to see Karen, Skovoola, and Estella.

"I have bad news," said Karen. "The film from your photo shoot is missing, and we don't have enough light to reshoot."

"I'm disappointed," said Barbie with a sigh. "But there will be other shoots, and I did have a wonderful time on the island."

She turned and waved good-bye to Herman the dolphin and headed back to the hotel with the others.

Three weeks later, Barbie was at home fixing lunch when the telephone rang. It was Karen.

"Hi, Barbie. Guess what," said Karen. "The *What's In* swimsuit issue has just been printed."

"Who's on the cover? Is it Laureen or Estella?" asked Barbie.

"Why don't you come down to the office and see for yourself," said Karen. "I'll give you a copy hot off the press."

A short while later Barbie hurried into the offices of *What's In*. The new edition was on display. Barbie couldn't believe her eyes.

"Oh, my goodness!" she exclaimed. "Herman and I are on the cover!"

Just then, the elevator opened. Barbie watched as Laureen walked into the reception area.

WHAT'S IN

Laureen's jaw dropped when she saw the cover. "Where did that picture come from?" she screamed.

"Skovoola took it at Dolphin Cove," said Barbie. "Isn't it funny how things work out? Skovoola never would have taken that picture of me if the other film hadn't disappeared!"